THE Bloody Water Bridge:
Book 1
By
Kiamesha Denise Sims

The Bloody Water Bridge Book 1

The Link Series, Volume 1

kiamesha denise sims

Published by kiamesha denise sims, 2024.

THE BLOODY WATER BRIDGE BOOK 1

First edition. August 30, 2024.

Written by kiamesha denise sims.

Also by kiamesha denise sims

A Short Story Collection
Targets: Book 1
The Boy And The Girl In The Tower: Book 1

Of The Infinity Duo
Blue Stars: Book 1

The Dark Night Of The Soul
The Dark Night Of The Soul: Book 1
The Dark Night Of The Soul: Book 2

The Link Series
The Bloody Water Bridge Book 1

Watch for more at https://kiameshadenisesims.wixsite.com/ website-1.

Table of Contents

For those who love listening to crime shows and podcasts so they can sleep. And for those that seek adventure but are not prepared for what they find.

Trigger warnings: contains nudity, profanity, murder, and gore

`The Bloody Water Bridge: Book 1:

Joanna Anderson sipped her coffee slowly, each drop a bitter caress against her lips, the dark liquid swirling like ink in the predawn silence of New York. The city around her was a restless beast, its heartbeat echoing through the veins of the streets, yet she remained still, wrapped in the quiet turmoil of her thoughts, the shadows around her thickening with every passing second.She wanted to relax and maybe get the chance to be a tourist but there was a call. Her job alarmed her at 3 AM. She left a note promising to call soon before she left.She followed the energy and was led to a house. She found her way in and scanned. "This is strange, it looks like a normal apartment,"

"What the hell are you doing in my house? You have three seconds to leave before I call the cops!" the owner grabbed a metal bat.

She bit her lip and slowly turned. "What the hell are you doing Steven?"

He eased. "Joanna, oh thank goodness!"

"Hi, it's been too long," she hugged him.

They sat down.

"Would you like something to eat or drink?" he asked.

"I'm sure I won't be here long," she insisted.

"Alright," he said. "What are you doing here?" he asked.

"I'm afraid I have concerns and *they* have some as well," she sighed.

"You're here on business then?" he asked.

"I am, and I don't want to be but I took the oath," she added.

"I understand but I took one as well," he answered.

She felt a stinging throughout her body. *There's magic here and it's overwhelming. Center yourself.*

"I'll have to report it, and it won't end well for both of us," she warned.

"I know," he said.

"Which is why I came with a warning," she said. "I want you safe, and everyone else too," she said. She clasped her hands in his. She was burning and her body ached and spasmed. As she drew a final breath, she had a prayer in her eyes and tears. A prayer for safety, redemption

"I know," he said.

Then it was over.

"But I took an oath," he kissed her forehead and close.

Chapter 2:

There were crickets around the dining room table. The air between Genevieve Violet Reins and her mother, Arianna, crackled with the tension of a storm about to break. The dining room, bathed in the dim, sickly glow of a single overhead light, felt like a battlefield where words were weapons, sharp and ready to cut deep. Silence hung between them, heavy and suffocating, as though the very walls conspired to trap them in this moment of unbearable stillness.

"Morning," her mother said.

"Hi," Genevieve smiled.

"Did you sleep alright?" her mother asked.

"I think so," Genevieve tried. "Did you sleep ok?" Genevieve asked.

"Yes," her mother answered. "Where's your father?" her mother asked.

"You don't want my clap back comment honestly, it's too early in the morning," Genevieve said.

"Gen, he pays the bills, makes sure we have a roof over our heads, and buys everything we could ever want," her mother said.

"I know, but he's never here!" Genevieve stormed off.

Genevieve pushed herself to the bus stop. Sometimes, Mom, you really piss me off.

"Miss, I need your seat, a wheelchair is boarding," the driver got Genevive's attention.

"Of course," Genevieve said.

The ride was long.

Genevieve slept throughout. When she arrived at her new school, it was pouring. Her body collided against someone under an umbrella.

He took off his jacket and placed it over her. "You're shivering," he said.

"Thanks," she said.

"No problem and I saw what you did on the bus," he said.

"You were following me?" she asked.

"I'm not a stalker, I go here too," he assured her.

"It was nothing," she brushed it off.

"It shouldn't be but it was," he said.

"What's your name?" she asked.

They came to the front doors of the school. He opened the door.

"Oh, thanks," she said.

"Welcome," he said."I'm William, by the way," he said.

"Genevieve," she said.

Arianna scrambled to work after a bagel and coffee. "Beth!'"

"What are you doing here?" Beth asked.

"Transfer," Arianna explained.

"How are things?" Beth asked.

"The same," Arianna sighed.

"Oh," Beth said.

"Can you show me around?" Arianna said.

"Sure," Beth smiled.

Steven was in a bar sulking after the victorious hype subsided.

"Steven, what the hell?" a friend asked.

"Who is that?" Steven asked.

"It's Victor, let's get you home," he sighed.

"Please don't tell Gen and Ari, they'll kill me," Steven begged.

"I won't, I've been there too," Victor said.

They got in the car.

Steven was knocked out in the back seats.

Victor dialed the office. "Lord, let him rest,"

The call went through.

"Hello?" Beth asked.

"Is this my assistant?" Victor asked.

"Yes, is there something you need?" Beth asked.

"Yes, I want the interns to get something for everyone to eat and drink, then the staff will meet in the boarding room, I need you guys to get to know each other," he instructed.

"Got it, will you be running late?" she asked.

"Yes, can you handle it until I get there?" he asked.

"I've got this but did you know that Arianna is back?" she asked.

"That's great," he hung up.

Beth smiled. Arianna and Sarah were standing by the door.

"Coffee run?" Arianna asked.

"Um, yes, I need your help and Sarah's as well," Beth said.

"Duty calls," Sarah grabbed notepads.

The trio went to the local coffee shop.

"I still can't believe you're back," Beth said.

"Me either, but Steven insisted," Arianna said.

"I know he's your husband and you love him, but you can say no," Sarah said.

"She's right," Beth said.

"You're both right," Arianna sighed.

"So, where are you from?" Sarah asked.

"Dayton, Minnesota," Arianna beamed.

"I grew up there, and I wanted to stay there but I guess it wasn't in the plan," Arianna remembered.

"Why?" Sarah asked.

"I got pregnant and married," Arianna explained.

"By Steven?" Sarah asked.

"Yep," Arianna said.

"How did you meet?" Beth asked.

"School, on the first day of freshman year, we dated, and I got pregnant and we got married," Arianna said.

"I was completely against it but I didn't want my church and family to disown me," Arianna sighed.

"Oh," Beth said.

"I swear Steven giving me Genevieve was the best thing he's ever done," Arianna added.

"What about you Sarah?" Beth asked.

"I grew up with a loving family and moved here after college," Sarah said.

"Ok," Arianna said.

"What about you Beth?" Arianna asked.

"Military kid and I even enlisted myself but was discharged after an injury," Beth said.

"Thank you for your service," Arianna smiled and they walked back to the office after getting what they needed.

Victor ate. Oh, they're gonna kill him for sure.

Steven came down the steps and ate. "They're going to kill me,"

"I know but how are you feeling?" Victor asked.

"Hungover," Steven said.

"After you eat, drink some water and maybe some Gatorade and then sleep it off," Victor instructed.

Victor grabbed his stuff.

"Steven settled on the couch. "Where are you going?"

"To work," Victor said.

In Dayton, Minnesota, a German grandma was making a birthday breakfast for her granddaughter. I can't believe she's 17 today. She placed the food on the dining room table. She knocked on her granddaughter's bedroom door.

"Come in," the voice answered.

Inside the room was slightly messy.

There was a young woman, Julia Carlson, shuffling through her closet.

"Honey, remember it's still September," her grandma said.

"You can be cozy, warm, and cute you know?" Julia answered.

"Fair enough, happy 17th, my sweet one," her grandma handed her a gift.

"What's this?" Julia ripped off the paper and patiently untied the bow. Inside was a moonstone bracelet. "It's like Mom's, thank you," she hugged her.

"It's your mother's; does it fit?" her grandma asked.

"Like a glove," Julia hugged her.

"I made breakfast, come along," her grandma said.

"What were my parents like?" Julia asked.

"They were a forbidden love, yet they were also a power couple," her grandma said. "Julia, they would be so proud of all you've become: you are a gorgeous and brainy woman," her grandma became teary.

"I hope so," Julia sat and ate.

"I'm sure Troy thinks so," her grandma smiled as Julia flushed.

"No fair!" Julia said.

"It was too easy," her grandma admitted.

Across the street lived Troy and his Dad, Peter Anderson. There was a smell of a fresh coffee pot and waffles with slightly burned bacon.Troy hid his folder of college information and applications into his backpack. These were liberal arts schools and as far away from home as possible. One day I hope he gets it. He placed the food on the table and went to the shower.After his shower he found his father walking in from work.

"Morning," Troy sat.

"Morning," his Dad yawned. "Why are there two plates out? Is your Mom home?" his Dad asked.

"No, Mom left a note, but I was hoping we could eat, " Troy said.

"Alright," his Dad sat.

"How was work?" Troy asked.

"The same," his Dad added.

"Oh OK," Troy said

"We're not one for small talk are we?" his Dad joked.

"Nope, but Mom sure is," Troy smiled.

"She is," his Dad agreed.

"Would you happen to know where she is?" Troy asked.

"At her job is all that I know," his Dad shrugged. "Does it say when she's coming home?" his Dad asked.

"No, but she says she'll call," Troy answered.

"Alright," his Dad said.

"Don't you think it's strange you don't know exactly what Mom's job is?" Troy asked.

"Yes, and I questioned her for years and she said she wants to tell me but she can't," his Dad said.

"Oh," Troy said.

There was a pause.

"There's something I want to discuss to you about my college," Troy said.

"Troy, we've discussed this, I won't allow it," his Dad said.

"Why? I've worked so hard!" Troy said. He stormed off.

"Troy-," his Dad said.

Troy circled around the neighborhood. Who the fuck does he think he is?! He took a deep breath after the walk. He headed to Julia's. "Morning, Carlson," he hugged her.

"What's wrong?" she hugged back.

He took a deep breath. "My Dad,"

"Let's sit for a second; are you hungry?" she asked.

"Even if I was, I am too "in it" to eat," he admitted.

"You're pretty warm, I'm gonna get a fan, water and a washcloth for your forehead," she said.

"Julia-," he said.

"Don't be silly," she stopped him

"Alright, can I lay on the couch?" he asked.

"Do ahead," her grandma spoke.

"Thank you," he said.

"It's time you make a move," her grandma hinted.

"I hear you," he said.

Julia's ear perked. Please make a move. She took a deep breath and came back. She kissed his forehead before placing the washcloth there. She plugged in the fan. She placed the water on the coffee table.

"You're too good to me, "Carlson," he sighed.

"Because you're always there for me, "Anderson," she smiled.

Her grandma beamed. They need to be dating; they are too adorable when they're together! "What are you doing for your birthday?" her grandma asked.

"Nothing," Julia said.

"Julia," her grandma sighed.

"Please this is what I want," she said.

"The usual: cake and ice cream and maybe a movie?" he asked.

"Sure, why not?" she asked. "Unless you will allow me to go to the bonfire this weekend?" she suggested.

"No!" her grandma projected her voice.

"It was worth a shot," Julia caved. "Are you sure you're not hungry?" Julia asked. "I have German pancakes, and it's loaded with love and yumminess, " Julia moved his feet and sat down next to him.

Troy sat up. "Alright," he took a piece. He closed his eyes and moaned.

"Right? They're so good!" she smiled.

His phone beeped. "We gotta go, we'll miss the bus if we don't hurry," he stood up.

"Right," she grabbed the containers and they headed out the door.

A few minutes later, Emily Rose was awakened from her sleep. A person stepped through beacons of light.

"Emmy?" the person asked.

"Joanna, it can't be true!" Emily Rose shrieked.

"I know you are grief-stricken but it's time for you to take my place and the prophecy is revealing itself," she spoke.

"I'm not ready," Emily Rose said.

"You are," Joanna smiled then the beacons disappeared.

There is a realm that was stuck in a time of chivalry. No buildings or businesses. Of kingdoms, open lands, and oaths.Three bells rang and boomed throughout. Friends that were separated answered the call and reunited in a forest.

"Mary!" Elizabeth smiled.

Mary curtsied and then embraced her. "Elizabeth, one of our own is dead,"

"I am aware and sadly it was Joanna," Elizabeth said.

"Her child and her husband...do you think they know?" Mary asked.

"I am not sure, we can ask Emily Rose if she arrives," Elizabeth said.

"There is no justice to be burned alive to death especially by a friend, they need to have stopped!" a voice said.

Two men arrived. On the right was Mary's first love, Oliver. On the left was Philip.

"My queen," Philip bowed.

"Philip, you've known me long enough to know that you are only allowed to call me that in front of my husband or anyone in royal," she rolled her eyes.

"Elizabeth, Mary, and Oliver; it's been too long," Philip tried again.

"Better, now come to hug us," Elizabeth smiled.

"I don't hug," Philip hesitated.

"Please," Mary said.

He embraced them.

"Elizabeth," Oliver said.

Elizabeth nodded.

"Mary, you look great," Oliver said

"Thank you, as do you," Mary curtsied.

"Where is the apprentice?" Philip asked.

"She has a grandchild to care for but I'm sure she'll be here, " Elizabeth said.

The friends walked to the river.

"Looking for me?" Emily Rose was soaked.

"Did you swim here?" Elizabeth asked.

"I had to," Emily fixed herself.

"Very well," Xavier whisked a wind to dry her off.

"Let's go," Mary led the way to the main castle.

The king, Ronald, was arguing with his spirited young daughter, Josalyn Rebecca Marie. Her height and her brutal tongue was no match for her father.

"Josalyn, do you need a spanking because I will not hesitate," her father barked.

"Fine, I'll behave," she caved.

"Good," he said.

She placed the food on the dining room table and sat.

"Where is your mother?" he asked.

"I think she had another meeting," she answered.

"I see," he said.

"I know that face, she's safe and it's quite incredible that women are protecting the realm and can be as powerful as men," she spoke.

"Josalyn-," he said.

"Don't cut me off, I was not born just to bear kids and submit to my husband!" she stormed out.

"Sometimes I forget that she's a mix of me and her mother until she's heated," he chuckled.

Josalyn went to do her studies at the library. Sure, she could've had tutors but she needed to trust her gut that this was the best for her. She walked and made it in half an hour. She walked inside and found that her teacher, Elias, was deep in the printed word. She knocked on the walk.

He tilted his attention up and beckoned her in.

"Good morning," she walked in.

"Princess Josalyn, why are you frowning?" he asked.

"Same reason," she sat and grabbed a quill and parchment.

"Ah," he said.

"I just don't understand," her face was in her hands.

"I know family misunderstands can be difficult, but please understand that you always will find someone who will," he said. "Come with me, you look like you need a walk,"

Elias and Josalyn went to the market.

"It's sunny here," she smiled.

"What are you doing for your birthday?" he asked.

"Oh, the usual: the royal protocol," she rolled her eyes.

"Am I invited?" he asked.

"Of course," she said.

"Good," he smiled. "Would you mind sneaking off?" he asked.

"Why?" she asked.

"Birthday surprise," he said.

"Oh, I hate surprises!" she sighed.

"It's a good surprise," he assured her.

"Why do we need all this food?" she asked.

"Because I'm running out," he admitted

"So, we did your grocery shopping?" she asked.

"Pretty much," he smiled.

Those eyes are so pretty and so calming to me. "Well, don't I feel used; you could've just left me there and came back,"

"You needed this walk anyway; plus your father would kill me if I left you alone," he said.

"You're right," she said.

"I wanted to be with you," he admitted.

"And why is that?" she was breathless.

"You are unlike any student I've ever met: so eager to learn, and so pretty as well," he said.

"Thank you," she said.

"You're welcome," he said.

"Can I get a hint?" she tried.

"Oh no," he chuckled.

"It was worth a shot," she said.

In a forest, there is a beautifully restored home that has been there since Xavier could remember.

This time when he returned from "hunting", he wasn't alone. He had a mini funeral for the animal he fed on and sighed. That never gets easier. He showered when he came back home, and then knocked on the door. He cracked the door and saw an angel in a deep slumber. "My poor Zoelle, I never wanted this to happen," He closed the door and walked to the kitchen to make something for her if she woke. It had been a week. He found a note and read it. He hurried to meet Mary, Elizabeth, Emily Rose, Oliver, and Philip.

Mary, Elizabeth, Philip, Xavier, and Emily Rose waited.

A few minutes later, Xavier arrived.

"Sorry, I'm late," Xavier sat with them.

"You're always late," Elizabeth brushed it off.

"I am so sorry Joanna isn't here, we would've loved seeing us together after all this time," Emily wept.

"I know how difficult this can be; are you sure you can do this?" Mary asked.

"It will be difficult I must admit, but it's an honor to and I believe it is what she would've wanted," Emily responded.

"If you need a second, we'll wait," Elizabeth said.

"Thank you," Emily said.

"Can we at least have a funeral for her?" Mary asked.

"Of course we can," Elizabeth said.

There was a minute of silence as they all looked at Elizabeth.

"Ronald has to agree, it's a tradition," Elizabeth responded.

"Does her husband and her son know?" Philip asked.

"No, but once they find out, they will be devastated and con-fused," Emily said.

"I know, which is why you have to tell them," Philip said.

"I will but slowly," Emily said. "So, it's really happening?" Emily looked around.

They nodded.

"We need to find her," Xavier mentioned.

"I know," Mary said.

"I feel so bad for the children," Mary wept. "If Emerson had to, without me..." she stopped.

Oliver walked over toward her. "I know, but you have us,"

"I wonder if he was still alive would he look or act like me or you and so many things," Mary responded to Oliver.

"Me too," he kissed her hair.

"He would've been 18 today," Mary wept.

"I can't imagine losing my granddaughter, Julia, she's healed me so much especially after my daughter just left and has never come back," Emily sighed.

"Has she asked about her Mom or Dad?" Mary asked.

"Every day; I tell her that they would be so proud of who she's become," Emily answered.

"Does she know?" Philip asked.

"No, because she'll tell Troy," Emily said.

"They're gonna find out and I think they'll appreciate it if they found out by someone they know," Elizabeth said.

"You're right," Emily realized.

"What new with everyone?" Philip asked.

"Well, Josalyn is definitely a mix of me and her father, I just hope that it doesn't scare any suitors away," Elizabeth sighed.

"The right man for her will come," Mary smiled.

"What about Elias?" Philip asked.

"She's her teacher and ten years older," Elizabeth said.

"They've known each other also, plus do you deny they have chemistry?" Xavier asked.

"No, fine I'll consider," Elizabeth sighed. "How is the business going?" Elizabeth asked.

"In the dumps," Philip sighed.

"Oh, I hope things turn around," Elizabeth said.

"Thank you," Philip said.

"Mary, would you like to come back?" Elizabeth asked.

"Sure," Mary said.

"I have a newborn, a female newborn," Xavier said.

"Oh, is she OK?" Mary asked.

"She hasn't woken up yet, but I'm not really concerned, everyone's reaction is different," Xavier continued.

"How did you meet?" Mary asked.

"At night," he stopped with a smile.

"Oh, now you play shy but happiness looks good on you," Philip said.

William was left at the counselor's office. Here we go. My dreams are coming true.

Genevieve was running to her homeroom. She sat in the back and was completely unnoticeable by the other students but by her teachers. She was that nerd: a hidden, yet open person with a bit of pessimism too.

"Good morning everyone," the teacher spoke.

There was a knock.

The guidance counselor came in and William was coming in after her.

"Everyone, this is William and I need a volunteer to show him around," she smiled.

There were no takers so she had to pick.

"Genevieve," the guidance counselor smiled.

"Me?" Genevieve asked.

"I think there's only one Genevieve in this class," William said.

"Please?" the guidance counselor asked.

"Sure?" Genevieve sighed. What did I just agree to? Her stuff fell off her desk. "Shit!"

William chuckled. "Need some help?"

Genevieve sighed and nodded.

"Here you go," he said.

"Great, thank you," the guidance counselor left.

The class officially began.

Arianna sighed.

The doors opened. He looked at her and smiled.

She smiled back. Damn, he ages like wine. This is awkward!

"Good morning everyone, I hope you enjoyed your coffee and treats," he said. "I really appreciate your patience. A friend of mine was in trouble," he explained.

Arianna sipped on her coffee. Same old Victor.

He passed out packets. "I want us to go through this,"

In Dayton, Troy and Julia were on the bus.

"Are you feeling any better?" she asked.

"I am, thank you, but you don't look so good," he noticed.

"Um... yeah, I just am a little dizzy," she said.

"I can take you back home, or the clinic," he said.

"No, I'm good," she said.

"I'm telling you that you're lying to me," he said.

He grabbed her bag.

"What are you doing?" she asked.

" I'm calling 911," he sighed.

"If you call...." she stopped and then she passed out.

"Julia-," he shook her.

"Yep," he dialed.

There was a phone call.

Emily Rose was resting but was woken up. "Hello?"

"It's Troy, something's wrong with Julia, she's out cold," he said.

"Where are you?" she jumped up and threw some clothes on. "Hello?" she asked.

"Hello?" he asked.

"Why isn't your phone charged?" he sighed.

"You need to hold her," the driver said.

"I wouldn't object to that," he smiled.

Julia opened her eyes. She was laying on lush, spring grass. She looked around her and saw she was surrounded by tall trees and the sky was a baby blue and transparent. "Where am I?" she wondered. "Julia, thank God and happy birthday," she heard a voice. She followed it and saw Troy's Mom smiling and they embraced. "It's so good to see you but where are we and how did I get here?"

"Walk with me," his Mom said.

"OK," Julia followed.

Troy was still holding Julia when Emily arrived.

"What happened?" she asked.

"We were talking and the next minute she was out," Troy explained.

"Are you the parent?" the EMT asked.

"Troy, she needs to be checked out, let her go," Emily sighed.

"Right," he said.

"Her pulse is faint and she's still breathing," the EMT stated. "We need to take her in," the EMT added.

"Troy, go to school and inform her teachers and get her assignments," Emily instructed.

"OK, but please keep me posted," he said. "I want you to fight whatever this is," he caressed her cheek and watched them disappear.

Emily sighed as they got into the ambulance and as they made it to the hospital. It's happening.

The doctor examined Julia. And did all the tests.

"She has iron deficiency anemia," "Her red blood cells have a decreased amount of hemoglobin which makes it hard for her body to circulate oxygen to her tissues, which probably caused her to pass out," the doctor said.

"Is that dangerous and what do we do about it?" her grandma asked.

"No, what she has is very common and I'm just happy we caught it," the doctor said. "I can prescribe a pill to take and you can eat things on this list, and please remember to schedule an appointment with her regular doctor,"

"Thank you," her grandma said.

Julia and Joanna walked.

"Honey, it's so good to see you," Joanna smiled.

"Where are we?" Julia asked. The very air here seemed to

hum with ancient secrets, the weight of unspoken stories pressing down on her shoulders.

"We are in the second realm," Joanna said.

"What are you talking about?" Julia asked.

"Your grandma didn't tell you?" Joanna asked.

"Tell me what?" Julia asked.

" Julia, it really isn't my place to tell you," Joanna sighed.

"Please," Julia said.

"There are two realms: here, a place that is stuck in time where magic and mystery reign, but there is also where you live, here it is known as the modern or the first realm," Joanna explained.

"OK," Julia said.

"I grew up here and so did your grandmother and your Dad," Joanna said.

"My Dad and my grandmother grew up here, it seems so serene why would they leave?" Julia asked.

"I'll let them answer that," Joanna said.

"How am I involved?" Julia asked.

"You and my son are involved because of... the impossible and what is possible," Joanna answered.

"I need you to go back," Joanna hugged her.

Julia opened her eyes and sighed. What the hell is going on? Why do I know that I've been lied to? She was discharged and couldn't talk.

"Is there a frog in your throat or something?" her grandmother made lunch.

"Nope; why are you lying to me?" Julia asked.

"Julia, what on Earth are you talking about?" her grandmother asked.

"Troy's Mom, she died and I saw her," she said.

"What did she tell you?" her grandmother stopped and froze.

"We met at the forest in the second realm and she told you and she that you grew up there with my Dad and to top it off Troy and I have this mission," she explained.

"Yes, she is dead and she is telling the truth," her grandma stated. "I wanted to tell you,"

"How am I supposed to handle this and keep this secret?" Julia went to her room.

Troy couldn't wait for the day to be over despite his short schedule as a senior. Is she OK? The day went by quickly and he was about to head home when he was told to give a message to Julia. He went home and relaxed a little. He did his work.

His Dad came in. He grabbed his phone. "Something's not right,"

"I'm worried too, but can you please chill a little her phone's either dead or she's sleeping," Troy said.

"You're right but by this time tomorrow I'm calling," his Dad responded.

"OK," he said.

"I'm surprised you're not at Julia's," his Dad said.

"She passed out on the bus this morning, I'm giving her space," he answered.

His phone beeped. He got a heavy jacket and an umbrella. "She's home and she wants to see me ASAP,"

"Make a move, it would be a birthday present that's long overdue," his Dad said.

Troy rolled his eyes and left.

Julia was outside.

"What the hell are you doing in the rain without boots, a jacket, or at least an umbrella?" Troy spotted her.

"There's no time for that," she protested.

"I'm not going anywhere with you until you get a heavy jacket and your umbrella," he crossed his arms.

"Fine," she went inside and returned. "Better?" she asked.

"Yep, so where are we going?" he asked.

"We're going to the bonfire spot," she said.

"OK," he said.

It took a few minutes but they were soon surrounded by trees, the natural Earth, and crisp air.

"It always smells amazing here after it's rained," he said.

"I know, it's so clean," she agreed.

"What happened this morning, you terrified me," he said.

"I have low iron," she said.

"Is that dangerous?" he asked.

"No, I can take a pill and then my levels should be normal," she assured him

"Thank goodness!" he sighed.

"Thank you, for worrying about me," she said.

"I'll always worry about you," he admitted.

"I mean we've been friends since birth," she said.

"Maybe more if you wanted," he said.

"I'll get back to you about that," she smiled.

They walked to a bench.

"I have something to tell you, but I'm not sure how you react and if you'll believe me," she said.

"It depends on what it is," he said.

"And I remember our vow: there are no secrets," she said.

"I know that you would have graduated in January," he said.

"Yes, I turned it down," she said.

"Why?" he asked. "This isn't because of me is it?" "Because I'm not going anywhere," he stated.

"Yes and no," she explained. "I want the whole high school experience, you can never get that back,"

"Julia, you turned down your dream school," he said.

"Troy, I can always reapply," she said.

"I understand," he said. "What else did you want to tell me?" he asked.

"Um... it's a lot," she said. "I don't know where to start," she admitted.

"Tell me what you know for sure then," he said.

"I know that our lives will change," she stated.

"I have to know now after you said that," he said.

"Troy Nicholas Anderson, I'm being serious!" she said.

"I know Julia," he said. "Are you sure you can't?" he asked.

"For sure," she said.

"OK," he said.

"I miss my Mom," he said.

"I know that too," she said. "I miss my Dad and my Mom, which is strange because I was a baby when they left," she said.

"Did you ever find out why they left?" he asked.

"No, but I have a theory which I can't tell you because of what I said earlier," she said.

"Darn you are so stubborn!" he said.

"That is accurate," she said.

"My Dad was freaking out about my Mom like usual," he said.

"Fuck!" she jumped up and paced.

"Are you alright?" he asked.

"No," she said.

"Honey, I need you to stop pacing," he said.

"No, Troy I can't lie to you but I have to," she said. "I mean I wanna tell you but it's your family and you'll be devastated and OMG!" she panicked.

"Julia, look at me, come here, I want you to sit please," he held her.

"Oh God," she shook and cried.

"Julia, it's OK," he said.

"No, it's not," she screamed.

"Julia, look at me, what on Earth is wrong; it usually me who's the mess," he asked

"Troy, I want to," she said.

"Are you sicker than what you're telling me?" he asked.

"No," she said.

"Julia, I need to take you home, you need to rest and it's getting too cold out here," he noticed.

"Troy I can't go home," she panicked.

"Why? Did something happen?" he asked.

"Troy, my grandma doesn't know I'm here," she said.

"Then we'll go to my house," he said.

"I can't go to your house either," she said.

"Julia, we can't stay here, please let me take you home," he grabbed her chin.

OK," she stood up and slipped.

"Honey, you can't walk, hold on," he dialed.

"Hello?" her grandmother answered.

"She's gonna scold me, but Julia and I are at the bonfire site and we were talking and she started panicking and now she can't walk," he sighed.

"Damn it Troy!" she said.

"Shut up Julia, I'm trying to help," he answered.

"Yes, she's yelling at you and she only does that when she's stressed," she hung up.

Her grandmother grabbed her car. I should've never unintentionally said that she shouldn't say anything. She knocked on Peter's front door.

"Joanna, thank God," he said.

"No, but I know where she is," she said.

"Where?" he asked.

"Come with me, we have a long drive to go get Troy and Julia," she sai

Chapter 3:

"Where is Joanna?" Peter asked.

"She's..." Emly stopped.

"So, they're gonna find her and who did this right because I filed one this morning," he said.

"Yes, they will and they're going to question you," she said.

"OK," he said.

"I'm so sorry," she said.

"Wait, how can you be so sure she's dead?" he asked.

"She visited me," she said.

"You can see the dead?" he asked.

"Yes, and she could sense energy shifts," she said.

"How would you know that?" he asked.

"We grew up together," she said.

"OK," he said. "Where are Troy and Julia?"

"They're in the forest although I've told them not to," she said.

"They're teenagers," he said.

"Good point," she said.

"Why didn't you want them there?" he asked.

"You can easily get lost there because there's something protecting it," she said.

"Magic?" he asked.

"You catch up first," she said.

"Yep," he said. "Do you know how she died?" he asked.

"She was hugged to death while she burned alive," she said.

"Jesus!" "Who would do this?" he asked.

"Sadly, it was one of her friends," she said. "She was trying to protect him and this happened," she said.

"I wanna-," he stopped and breathed in.

She sighed. "I know I wanna kill him too,"

"Thank you for telling me, now how am I going to tell Troy?" he wondered.

Julia wept.

"They'll be here soon," he wiped her tears.

"That's not why," she answered.

"What is it?" he asked.

"Wildfire," she said.

"You're lying," he said.

"I wouldn't lie about this," she said.

A car pulled up.

Troy's Dad stepped out.

"Is Mom dead?" Troy asked.

"Get in the car," his Dad instructed.

"Julia, I'm sorry I should've never asked that of you," her grandma said.

"You really shouldn't have," Julia agreed.

"Is my Mom dead?" he asked.

"She is," his Dad said.

"I can't-," he said before drifting off.

Genevieve looked at the clock and then heard the bell.

William stood up and walked to her desk. He waited. "Ready?"

"As ready as I'm ever gonna be," she answered.

"OK," he said.

"Follow me," she said.

"Where are we going?" he asked.

"The assembly," she led the way to the auditorium.

The place was crowded.

"This campus is huge, it takes up a whole street all the way around," he said.

"We share the campus with five other schools you know?" she sat.

"I wasn't aware," he responded. "You keep looking at me, is something on my clothes or my face or is my fly open?"

"No, I would tell you that, but your energy is refreshing," she said.

"In a good way?" he asked.

"Why?" she asked.

"I've figured out that too much of a good thing can be lethal too," he responded.

"So, who's on the stage?" he asked.

"The principal, the vice-principal, and the guidance counselor," she said.

"What do you really think about them?" he asked.

"Well, except for the guidance counselor, they make it harder to be at a college prep school," she said.

"You're being too polite... tell me," he waited.

"The king is on the right, the king's lackey is next and the beautiful kind maiden is next to the lackey," she laughed.

"Lackey...?" "Damn girl what did he do?" he laughed. I never knew she had such a colorful, blunt and cutthroat vocabulary

"Oh, he acts as if he owns us when in reality if it wasn't for our parents he wouldn't have a mission," she said.

"Remind me to never get you mad," he answered.

"I just did," she said.

"Genevieve Violet Reins is a mouthful," he said.

"You read my file?" she asked.

"She dropped it and I saw it when I picked it up," he said.

"You should ask for the organization job," she said.

"Why are you saying it as if you hated it?" he noticed.

"Nothing passes by you huh?" she asked.

"Like a shark smells blood," he joked.

"A nightmare," "I did it in my last school so I'm done with community service," she explained.

"Yet you still showed me around, so thank you," he said.

"You're welcome," she punched his arm.

"Ouch," he rubbed his arm.

"Sorry, sometimes, I forget my own strength," she admitted.

"It's ok," he said.

"Walk with me," she instructed.

"Where are we going?" he asked.

"The classes through the day and then I have a surprise," she smiled.

"I have a feeling you're full of surprises," he smiled.

"Unpredictable is more like it," she corrected him.

"Lead the way then," he said.

The next few classes swarmed by and soon the day was finally over.

"So, where are we going?" he asked.

"Follow me if you want to find out," she smiled.

They took the bus and sat next to each other.

Genevieve texted her Mom. I need some space. Going back to my safety net. Don't worry, I'm not alone. See you soon. She soon found her way to rest.

William smiled. Aww, she's knocked out. It was probably too much for her. She looks so peaceful.

They arrived and walked around. The place was empty. They sat on the grass.

"Where are we?" he asked. The very air here seemed to hum with ancient secrets, the weight of unspoken stories pressing down on her shoulders.

"Welcome to my paradise," she smiled.

"It's serene, so different from the city," he said.

"I think the same way," she sat.

"Can you swim?" he asked.

"No," she said.

"How is that? "You live by a lake," he waited.

"I lean towards the apple picking," she responded.

"The sun is shining on you," he smiled.

"It's shining on you too," she smiled back.

"Do you trust me?" he asked.

"That depends, should I?" she asked.

"I think you can but I understand why you might not... at least not right away," he said.

"Thank you, for understanding Will, now what did you want me to try?" she asked.

"I want you to lie back and close your eyes," he said.

"OK," she leaned back.

"Feel the sun and the wind and maybe the ground underneath you," he instructed. "You can put your arms by your sides or even your hands over your heart, on your chest or on your belly," he added.

She sighed. Peace and quiet. Why can't it be like this all the time?

"What's it feel like?" he asked.

"It feels whole," she smiled.

"You can feel that all the time, no matter what, even if you're in this environment or not," he said.

"You think so?" she asked.

"I know so," he said. "Can I hold your hand?" he asked.

"OK," she said.

He tapped my hands. Stroking them slow then in circles. "Your hands are so rough,"

"What is that tingling?" she asked.

"My energy," he said.

"Our energy is mixing and you're hesitating," he said.

"I'm not used to peace always being with me, that's why," she responded.

"Everyone deserves to know peace," he smiled.

Time passed by and soon, they fell asleep side by side.

Genevieve hummed and opened her eyes. She grabbed her phone. "Oh, no, I need to go home," she said.

"I can walk you home, my house is that way anyway," he said.

"Thanks," she said.

"Let's go," he said.

Arianna, Sarah, and Beth sighed as the day ended.

"Want me to drive you guys home?" Beth asked.

"Are you sure?" Arianna asked.

"Yep, I'm in no rush, I live alone," Beth insisted.

"Oh Ok, but what if your house is before ours?" Arianna asked.

"It's no trouble and again I live alone," Beth said.

"Alright," Arianna got in.

"That's so kind of you, thanks, Beth," Sarah got in.

Beth started the car. "Who knew that the meeting would be so long and the day would be so busy?"

"Well, he wanted us to have a productive day, it's just how he is," Arianna shrugged.

"You would know this, how?" Sarah asked and raised an eyebrow while they waited for an answer.

"He was my first heartbreak, but I always wished him well," Arianna sighed.

"First serious boyfriend?" Beth asked.

"Yes, in fact, I wanted my first time to be with him," Arianna gasped. And then she blushed and sighed.

"First ex too?" Sarah asked.

Arianna nodded.

"Aww, sweetie, that must've been rough, why did you break up?" Beth asked.

" he said it was selfish for him to let me wait for him even though I was willing to," " "I never thought I'd see him again," Arianna continued.

"You did and you will," Sarah smiled.

"I know," Arianna smiled.

"What if this is your second shot at a romance?" Sarah beamed.

"This is not a rom-com, he's my boss that's all," Arianna

protested.

"If you could and Steven wasn't in the picture, I bet you would," Beth smiled.

"Whatever!" Arianna said.

"You can't hide your feelings forever, especially not those," Sarah commented.

"So, Sarah, any ex drama we need to worry about?" Arianna teased.

"Nope, I did date a stripper once," Sarah admitted.

"Really, you don't seem like the stripper type?" Arianna jokes.

"I proved you wrong," Sarah said.

"What about you Beth?" Sarah asked.

"Chasity after cheating BS," Beth said.

"Girl, I salute you!" Arianna said.

"Would you happen to have that stripper's number?" Beth asked.

"Why?" Sarah asked.

"Relax, it's if we need a girl's night," Beth said.

"Good because I call dibs and you have to at least wait until we break up and I'm over him," Sarah stated.

"Noted," Beth said.

"She's right," Arianna sighed.

"What's wrong?" Sarah asked.

"I forgot what it's like to feel," Arianna said.

"Well, we're here if you ever need us," Sarah saw her house, told Beth to pull over and she smiled at them before stepping out of the car.

Arianna was silent. She was choked, cornered, and cowered. Is this what Genevieve feels every day?

"Are you OK?" Beth asked.

"I will be," Arianna answered.

"I know but right now you aren't," Beth noticed.

"My house is right here," Arianna suffered and sniffed.

Beth parked. She took a deep breath. "Ari, come here,"

Arianna stiffed the moment by pulling away.

"Ari, can I hug you: like a bear hug?" Beth asked.

Arianna nodded. She gripped Beth and screamed so hard she began to shake.

"I know," Beth said. "But you're going to make it,"

"How?" Arianna asked.

"I just know you will, do you want me to pick you up tomorrow?" Beth asked.

"I have to drive Genevieve to school, I will meet you guys there," Arianna cleared her throat.

"Alright," Beth answered and drove off.

Arianna walked into her home. Why is this so damn hard?

Steven came in soon after her. "Hi,"

"Where have you been and have you been drinking?" she asked.

"Nice to see you too," he snapped.

"I just want to make sure you're OK," she tried again.

"I'm not OK and yes, I've been drinking," he admitted.

"Oh, Steven what is going on with you? "You're barely home and your addictions are back," she asked.

"Ari-," he walked away.

"Please talk to me," she begged.

Genevieve walked in.

Will stood by the door. "See you tomorrow?"

"Where else would I be?" she asked.

"I have a few ideas actually," he said.

"Write them down and we'll discuss," she smiled, walked in, watched him disappear, and then closed the door.

"Hi, Mom and...Dad great, how long are you going to be back?" she wondered.

"Genevieve Violet Reins..." her Dad said.

"Whatever," she went to her room.

Genevieve got comfy and started her homework. After that, she went through her bag. A note was there. Tu sei leggero, non importa cosa :) -William.

Troy slept during the car ride. He walked into his home with his Dad. They were both gruesomely silent that it was eerie. No words would come or bring her back, possibly not even heal.

Troy walked into his room and destroyed everything. His phone rang. "Hi, Carlson,"

"Troy, there are no words so I just wanted you to know if you need anything...at any time-," she said.

"Just stop," he said.

"Too mundane?" she asked.

"And cringy," he added.

"I'm not mad at you Julia," he said. "I just didn't want to believe you,"

"I know," she said.

"Julia, are you crying?" he asked.

"I am because I can't imagine what it's like to lose someone so dear to you," she explained.

"Listen to me it's not your fault at all," he wept too.

"At least we can cry together," she begged.

"That's my girl," he smiled.

Troy's Dad sighed. My heart is gone. How can I raise Troy?

We are so strained. How can I be a better person... a better man?

After the phone call, Julia and Troy hung up.

Julia coughed. "I really needed that," She wiped her tears. She did her homework and took a shower. Then she tried to relax until bed.

Emily Rose sighed. Is it always going to be this hard? They're just children in an adult situation and it's completely unfair.

Back in the second realm, the day has ended.

A community of misfits was trained in chaos, pain, and melancholy. They were recruits once and maybe one day they would uprise and train the next recruits.

Each had a bunker with one door and a window that was barred. The room was dark and the only light was a candle.

An eighteen-year-old was drumming his fingers. He was sore from today's workouts and back to back training without any breaks. He needed warm water and something to soothe the pain. You would think I'd be used to this by now.

The door slid open. Standing there was another recruit. He looked like he was put through the wringer and it seemed worse than the eighteen-year-olds.

"What the hell do you want, Conor?" the eighteen-year-old asked.

"Hmmm... grumpy, can I come in?" the recruit asked.

"Make it quick," the eighteen-year-old sat up.

The recruit walked in and sat. "Happy birthday, Emerson," he handed over a paper and with a blue ribbon.

"Thank you, what is it?" Emerson asked.

"I got your answers," Conor answered and went back to his bunker.

Emerson slid the ribbon off and put it under the candlelight.

"He found my birth link,"

Chapter 4:

Genevieve dreamt. She never dreamt. She was naked completely at the summit of the day. She was in a forest. It seemed her surroundings were blinding. Its intensity was stronger than the sun. Where is this beautiful place and why am I here? She went deeper into the forest and saw that there was a hammock flying under a waterfall. She stepped into the waterfall and the water felt so cleansing.

There was a whistle in her earshot.

A ladder flew down from the hammock and she climbed it with no hesitation.

"Wow, this view is amazing!" she laid down.

Like a thunderclap, someone swung on a vine and she saw this.

He landed a few feet in front of her. "Hi, there,"

"Oh geez," she shielded herself.

He tossed her clothes.

"Turn around," she said.

He did.

She changed. "Alright, you can look, and thanks for the clothes," she said.

"You're welcome, "Origin," he said.

"My name is Genevieve," she said.

"Sorry, Genevieve it is; I'm Conor," he apologized.

"Now that the introductions are over what do you want?" she asked.

"Ouch, that hurt, what if I don't want anything?" he asked.

"Everyone wants something," she replied.

"Fair enough, what do you want?" he asked.

"I don't know," she answered.

"Alright, next question," he waited.

"How did you know I wanted to ask something?" she asked.

"You have that curiosity," he explained.

"And it killed the cat," she added.

"I don't understand," he waited.

"Curiosity can cause conflict and destruction... trust me," she explained.

"I see," he said.

"So, where are we?" she asked.

"The second realm," he said.

"Never heard of it," she shrugged.

"You will," he said. "Give me your palm," he said.

"Will it hurt?" she hesitated.

"No," he assured her. He traced a crescent moon on both sides of her palms.

It was silver and sparkly even after a few minutes.

"Consider it a welcome present," he smiled.

"Do you have one too?" she asked.

"It's under my ribs on both sides," he answered.

"Cool," she said.

"That view from the hammock is amazing!" she beamed.

"I agree," he said.

"You look tired," he lifted her up and they flew.

He laid her down and kissed her forehead. "Rest Genevieve, and I'm so glad to see you,"

Genevieve opened her eyes in the morning. "That was the nicest and most confusing dream I've ever had,"

"Morning Gen," her Dad said.

"You're still here?" Genevieve asked.

"I'm not going anywhere," her Dad said.

"We'll see," she poured cereal.

Her Mom came running down the steps. "My alarm,"

"Sit down love, you need a break," her Dad said.

"You did the laundry and made breakfast?" her Mom asked.

" I'm so sorry how I treated you guys," "Can you forgive me?" he asked.

"Dad, there are days where I am so pissed and worried but you're on probation," Genevieve decided.

"You've got a lot to prove," her Mom agreed.

"I gotta go," Genevieve said.

"Have a great day," her Mom said.

"You too," Genevieve smiled. Someone's finally listening!

Arianna finished. "I gotta go to work," she said.

He grabbed her and sat her on the counter. He kissed her deeply and passionately. With his hands going down her back.

Then she pulled away, and she shivered. "I gotta go to work,"

"OK then," he smiled.

Arianna called Beth. "Can you pick me up?"

"Sure, I'll be there in ten," Beth waited as Sarah got in the car and buckled up.

"Good morning, and thank you for picking me up; are we going to pick up Arianna as well?" Sarah asked.

"Good morning to you too and yes we are," Beth answered.

"Cool," Sarah yawned. "Want to get some coffee after we pick up Arianna?"

"We really have to slow down on the coffee but sure," Beth said. "How was your night?"

"It was the same, what about you?" Sarah asked.

"Me too," Beth answered.

They pulled up to Arianna and Arianna got in the car. She

buckled up. "Mornin,"

"Hi, how are you feeling?" Beth asked.

"I don't know," Arianna shrugged.

"Out with it; what has caused you to be so indecisive?" Sarah asked.

"Steve's home," Arianna explained. "Genevieve and I are so happy to see him but I'm afraid we feel like he's a stranger,"

"Don't speak for her," Sarah warned.

"I'm not, she tells me this all the time, but I think she believes I don't listen to her," Arianna admitted.

"Do you listen to her?" Beth asked.

"Maybe not," Arianna sighed.

There was a long silence.

"So, basically he's on thin ice," Beth spoke.

"Yep," Arianna agreed

"Let him prove himself," Sarah suggested.

They got their coffee and breakfast. Then they headed to work.

Steven was caught in his thoughts as he decided to clean up the house. She was someone's child, wife, mother, and my best friend. I was selfish. I was stupid. Regardless, she tried to help me anyway. Now she's dead and it's my fault. He winced as the mark on his arm sparkled a shock as a reminder: It's us or them.

Troy went back home to shower, eat, and get ready for school after a run. After that, he found his father still in only his underwear. "How are you feeling?"

"Why do you care? We don't talk anyway,"

"I lost her too you know but I am not going to be spoken to that way," Troy responded and left.

Julia showered and packed her bag. Before she went to eat,

she put on her Mom's bracelet. This is a new day. She walked downstairs and ate. She found a note under the container. EAT AND TAKE YOUR MEDS. I HAD TO GO BUT I'LL BE BACK. REMEMBER TO LOCK THE DOOR BEFORE YOU LEAVE. HAVE A GOOD DAY. -GRANDMA. "OK," she shrugged. She finished up, took her meds, and left for school after locking the door.

Emily Rose walked around as she waited for her damp clothes and shoes to dry. She found herself in a small village where she grew up. She smiled and then sighed. I'd never thought I'd be back here," Now, it's just an empty field that's clearly been burnt down. Over there was the well where we would get water. And there was where the pastors would give wisdom to anyone who would listen. And if you kept going in my direction, there was a marketplace.

"Emily Rose?" she heard.

"That's me," she stopped.

"It's great to see you, I am Loreley's eldest," the woman spoke. She was holding baskets of clothes, needles, and another with food.

"Layla," Emily Rose said.

They embraced.

"Wow, you've grown, you're a spitting image of your mother," Emily Rose said.

"Thank you, may she rest in peace," Layla said.

"How is your father?" Emily Rose asked.

"He's with my Mom," Layla sighed.

"Where is your brother?" Emily Rose asked.

"I don't know, he's been gone for days," Layla explained. "I'm scared because that's not like him," Layla was saddened.

Emily sighed. "I hope he comes back safely,"

Layla agreed. "I've looked everywhere I can think of and even those places where he wouldn't go, and it's like he disappeared,"

"Keep the faith, my dear," Emily Rose advised.

"I will," Layla eased.

They went their separate ways.

Xavier smiled. He was holding Zoelle's hand tightly. She moaned and made slight movements. Her eyes opened soon after. "Xavier?"

He kissed her palm. "I'm here, how are you feeling?"

"Like I haven't eaten in days," she responded.

"Well, you haven't, but at least you got quality sleep," he said.

"Always the jokester," she smiled.

"I was extremely nervous, I thought I lost you," he said.

She sat up and threw her arms around him. "I missed you too,"

Philip saw a female goat and she was giving birth. Soon a lamb was born and snuggled against its mother. He tended to his chores and saw his son, Elijah. "No lessons today?"

Elijah helped his father. "No, it's the day of Josalyn's birthday party; and there's plenty of preparation to do,"

"Are you going?" his father asked.

"I wouldn't miss it for anything in this world," Elias smiled.

"Aww, would you court her if you had the chance?" his father asked.

"Yes, but I am her teacher and 10 years her senior," Elias said.

"So, if you like her that much are you willing enough to try?" his father pondered.

"I am," Elias stated.

"It's settled then, I will speak to her parents," his father said.

"Is that a newborn?" Elias asked.

"It is, I believe it's a girl," his father said.

"Can we name her Gwenth after Mom?" Elias asked.

"That's so wonderful, you truly have her heart, but you look just like me," his father smiled.

"Can we talk about her?" Elias asked.

"Of course, we can," his father led them inside.

They ate.

"Your mother was completely out of my league," his father reminisced.

"You're kidding!" Elias's eyes widened.

"Absolutely not," his father laughed. "I knew that I wanted her, so I pursued her and thank God we ended up together," "She was a beautiful woman but very poor," "She studied very hard to improve her rank; she met me and we just fell in love,"

"How did you propose?" Elias asked.

"I said that there was one present left and it was a picture of her saying "forever out of my league," his father smiled. "I've never seen her so shocked but she had that look that I knew she wanted me too,"

"She picked your name because she said that she always wanted to name her son after her mentor as a thank you for all of her hard work," his father explained.

"Mom," Elias remembered. "I think Josalyn reminds me so much of Mom,"

"I can see that," his father agreed.

Josalyn sighed. I can't wait for these lessons to be over! To have a future with my (possible) husband so these can stop! Even if I don't end up with anyone I have an extra skill under my belt.

She rested after changing. She was woken up by something soft landing on her side. She smiled and saw that it was a pot of sunflowers. I thought you may need it and like these. -Elias. "That man is a Godsent!" she blushed.

Mary remembered. Happy birthday, Emerson. I want you to know how much we love you.

Elizabeth saw Mary in her room and followed her. She sat. She smoothed Mary's hair out of her red and puffy eyes. "Another nightmare?"

Mary sighed. "No, but it never gets easier,"

"I can only imagine losing my only child who I carried for nine months, had a day and a half of brutal labor, and for him to be taken before you even get to hold him," Elizabeth remembered.

"I got cheated," Mary decided.

Elizabeth got into Mary's bed and spooned her. "I know,"

Ronald was looking for Elizabeth. He saw it all. Well..this is not... Elizabeth is mine!

Oliver sat. Happy birthday, my boy. Your mother and I love you so much.

Arianna walked into her office. She began to work and found her pace between coffee sips.

There was a knock on her office door.

"Come on in," she said.

"Arianna, you can take your eyes off the screen, the document isn't going anywhere," they said.

"True, is there something you need?" she asked.

"Well, first off I need you to turn that chair around," they answered.

"Who is it?" she asked.

"Victor," he answered.

"There's that dominating part of the boss persona," she joked.

"I'm dominating all the time, but in a gentle and playful way," he responded.

"Right," she rolled her eyes.

"It's true," he said.

"Is there something you need?" she asked.

"I wanted to talk, it's about Steven," he said.

"Why is that your concern?" she asked.

"Easy tiger, I just wanted you to know that I saw him at the bar and took him to my place so he could sober up, what's going on he can't tell anyone and it's eating him up," he explained.

"And you know this how?" she listened with intention and more attention now.

"Because I was once in his shoes," he said.

"OK, is there anything you wanna share or want from me?" she asked.

"Yes, come with me," he said.

"I have work to do," she said.

"You have three seconds or I will throw you over my shoulder," he warned.

"So?" she protested.

"Backwards," he stressed.

"I'm coming," she sighed.

They walked to the meeting room.

"Where is everyone?" she asked.

"No idea," he answered.

They walked inside and everyone else jumped out. "Happy birthday!"

"I should've known you had that grin as we got closer to this meeting room," Arianna stated.

"Want some cake?" Sarah asked.

"I'd love some," she eagerly took the plate.

Steven took a nap but it wasn't pleasant. He saw Joanna.

She was limb and looking like she was still crying.

He tried to look away but it was like some force was holding his body forcing him to look. He jumped into his sleep. *This is gonna be a long life if I can't let this go.*

Chapter 5:

The next morning was crowded with drama.

It began in the second realm, and Emerson was woken up by the barks of his commander.

"I'm coming," Emerson rubbed his eyes. He hurried but was caught by racing thoughts. *This changes everything. I have an actual lineage but why was I given up?*

The commander waited. "Good morning, recruit 30078, I have news,"

"News?" Emerson asked.

"I have a mission for you, I believe you're ready," the commander explained.

"What is it?" Emerson asked.

"Have you heard of the "Origins?" the commander asked.

"Of course, I have," Emerson said.

"Good, your mission is to find the Origins and then convince them, and if not destroy them," his commander instructed.

"OK," Emerson said.

Conor jumped up. "Something's not right," He felt intense shifts and it made his stomach turn. Regardless, he followed it. *Why am I always a hero? Why can't I mind my own business?*

He knocked and was invited in.

"I got my first mission," Emerson beamed.

"Congrats, what is it?" Conor asked.

"Find the Origin and do what we usually do," Emerson shrugged.

"Emerson, please you can't-!" Conor winced.

"Emotion is weakness, recruit 7001, you will handle your ultimate punishment but at the maximum," the commander stated.

"Fine, but you are making a mistake," Conor's head hung low

as he was carried to his fate.

Emerson grabbed his belongings. I'm out of here.

Genevieve yawned in the shower. She washed and noticed her palms on both sides were sparkling. There were the same crescents from her dream. She wiped her eyes several times and rinsed her hair before stepping out, drying herself, returning to her room to get ready for another day. She hummed and heard several hums matching her too as well as glides. These glides were in a never-ending cycle. Some would overlap. There were glances and a pass of the energy going onward. It was a ritual done with great pride.

Just like that, she was brought back.

Conor felt a slashing of sorts. "Stop!"

"Toughen up," the commander smirked.

After a while, he blacked out.

Genevieve heard screams and crackling of thunder."Don't you dare touch him!"

Everything around her was hit by an excellent force and shattered.

"Genevieve, what the hell did you just do?" her father asked.

"I need to go to school," she walked out the door. What the hell did I just do? She found herself on the bus and knocked out.

"Genevieve, we're here," she was woken up from her rest.

"Where?" she asked.

"School?" We're on the bus," he answered.

"William, how did I get on the bus?" she asked.

"Girl, you need coffee and at least a donut, you look like death," he helped her off the bus, into the school, and to the cafeteria.

"I'm not hungry," she protested.

"Eat anyway," he slid a piece over.

She took a bite and hummed and smiled. "OMG,"

"Welcome back, what the hell is going on with you?" he asked.

"Coffee," she smiled.

"I can get more," he sighed.

"You might have to throughout the day," she hinted.

"I can do that, what happened?" he asked.

"I woke up this morning with these," she pulled up her sleeves.

"I don't see anything," he said.

"I have tattoos," she said.

"What are they?" he asked.

"Wildfires?" she pondered. No, that's not it.

"You had a very long night, I see and maybe you need to slow down on the coffee," he grabbed the cup and it spilled all over him.

"I need this coffee," she grabbed the other.

He grabbed the other and caught her wrist instead. "Geez, your pulse, I need to get you a nurse,"

But there's a bunch of wildfires out there, we need to help them," she whined.

"You can't help them if you're in a bed," he helped her to the nurse's office.

"What's all this?" the nurse asked.

"I don't know, but something's not right," he explained.

"Bucket?" she whined.

"Here you go," he held it out.

"Her pulse is way too high," the nurse stressed.

"Genevieve, did you take something?" he asked.

"No, I did not, but I need more coffee," she said.

"No, more coffee," he stressed.

"Dear, can you tell me who we can call?" the nurse said.

"My Mom's at work," she responded.

"What's wrong?" he asked.

"I have no idea but she needs to go get checked out now," the nurse dialed her Mom and then 911.

Arianna was typing away when she got the call. She dialed Victor. "I need to go see Genevieve, she's going to the emergency room,"

"Go, I understand," he sighed. I am so sorry that this is happening. And to think I had to fight to get out. I'm glad I did. Innocence or guilty we have no right to take justice in our own hands.

Steven gasped. "Not my baby girl," He hastily dialed a number for help. "Victor, I need your help,"

Victor looked at his watch. "Meet me in the front at noon,"

"I can be there now," Steven dressed.

"You can't Arianna still doesn't know," Victor said.

"Damn it," Steven slammed the phone on the receiver.

Arianna was pulled aside by the doctor that saw Genevieve at the hospital. "What's happened?"

"Coffee," he laughed.

"You're saying that she drank too much coffee," she had to laugh in relief.

"Caffeine in high doses can be dangerous," he said.

Genevieve tossed and turned. She was way too big for the bed and was stretched out. Even her gown had to be doubled up and be pinned to not expose her body. Her arm hung low and limb.

Arianna sat down. "Since when does she have a tattoo?"

Genevieve saw Conor. He was gagged, dirty, and bruised. She rushed toward him. "Oh, hell no," she set him free.

"Genevieve, you need to get out of here," he warned.

"But you're hurt," she refused.

"I said now," he led her to a secret closet that led outside.

"Conor, you don't need to be the hero," she ran back.

"I know, but it's neither of our faults," he winced.

"Conor," she held him up.

"Remember that it's not your fault when that door opens," he begged.

"We can both go," she tried. "Please-," she said.

"No, Genevieve, promise me," he said.

She sighed and went back into the closet.

Don't miss out!

Visit the website below and you can sign up to receive emails whenever kiamesha denise sims publishes a new book. There's no charge and no obligation.

https://books2read.com/r/B-A-OCHN-EJRXE

BOOKS 2 READ

Connecting independent readers to independent writers.

Did you love *The Bloody Water Bridge Book 1*? Then you should read *Crimson Blue Blossom*[1] by Katherina Star!

[2]

Love, adventure, bravery, and tragedy cradle an alternative magical society. When its university opens up and strangers with linked ancestors meet the past comes to the light.

Read more at https://katherinastarbooks.us/.

---

1. https://books2read.com/u/4A58Mp

2. https://books2read.com/u/4A58Mp

Also by kiamesha denise sims

A Short Story Collection
Targets: Book 1
The Boy And The Girl In The Tower: Book 1

Of The Infinity Duo
Blue Stars: Book 1

The Dark Night Of The Soul
The Dark Night Of The Soul: Book 1
The Dark Night Of The Soul: Book 2

The Link Series
The Bloody Water Bridge Book 1

Watch for more at https://kiameshadenisesims.wixsite.com/website-1.

About the Author

I am a young woman, an optimist yet I can very pessimistic some-times. I am stubborn, driven, a romantic, a writer, and an author. I grew up with cerebral palsy and it was a struggle. I always had to prove myself and work harder than others just to do "normal" things. I was (kind of still am)mousy, a people pleaser. I made the best of it one achievement after the next, an actor on the stage. People knew of me but they didn't really know me. It's lonely.

That's why I starting writing. ___I wanted a connection. I wanted hope despite everything around me. I wanted real friends and love. I wanted a purpose.___

I started at age 10 with short stories. I read those back and they were definitely cringe-worthy fanfiction. Then they just got longer, deeper, soothing, healing. I was home. I decided this is what I wanted to do for the rest of my life and to share them despite being scared like hell.

If I give hope or make someone dig deep within themselves and feel safe then I am a happy camper!

Read more at https://kiameshadenisesims.wixsite.com/web-site-1.

About the Publisher

www.ingramcontent.com/pod-product-compliance
Lightning Source LLC
Chambersburg PA
CBHW021759150726
47989CB00004B/1721